ABDO Publishing Company is the exclusive school and library distributor of Rabbit Ears Books.

Library bound edition 2007.

Library of Congress Cataloging-in-Publication Data

Metaxas, Eric.
  Puss in boots / written by Eric Metaxas ; illustrated by Pierre Le-Tan.
      p. cm.
  Summary: An adaptation of the Perrault tale in which a clever cat secures the fortune of
his rather dimwitted young owner.
  ISBN-13: 978-1-59961-311-6
  ISBN-10: 1-59961-311-5
  [1. Fairy tales. 2. Folklore—France.] I. Le-Tan, Pierre, ill. II. Puss in Boots. English.
III. Title.

PZ8.M85Pu 2006
398.2 0944'04529752—dc22
[E]

                                                                          2006042595

All Rabbit Ears books are reinforced library binding
and manufactured in the United States of America.

ABDO
Publishing Company

Puss in Boots

Written by Eric Metaxas ❧ Illustrated by Pierre Le-Tan

Rabbit Ears Books

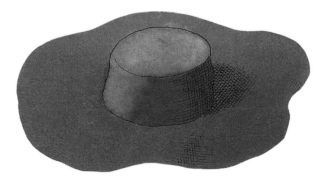

*O*nce upon a time, in the wine region of Carabas in France, there lived a miller and his three sons. All that the miller possessed in the entire world were his mill, his donkey, and his tomcat. But the mill was in fine shape, the donkey did a splendid job of turning the millstone, and the old tomcat—well, he had done such a stupendous job of keeping the mice out of the grain that no one had seen a single mouse in the area for many years.

When the miller died he bequeathed his eldest son the mill, he bequeathed his middle son the donkey, and to his youngest son, Claude, he bequeathed the aforementioned kitty, who had already begun to enjoy an early retirement.

Of course, the father had assumed quite naturally that the three brothers would operate the mill together and he had only bequeathed them the mill, the donkey and the tomcat respectively, as a formality. ✤ But the two older brothers, seeing there was no longer any use for the cat, decided to conspire against their younger brother and take his share of the mill for themselves.

✤ "Take your shaggy inheritance and be off!" they said, pointing to the cat. "And don't spend him all in one place!" ✤ With that they sent Claude on his way.

eedless to say, he was terribly upset. "My poor father thought I would be provided for," thought Claude, "and now all I have is a miserable tomcat! If only Papa knew! Oh, woe is me! Woe is me!" ✦ "Woe is you!?" thought the cat. "What about me? Imagine! I did such a good job killing all the mice that I became obsolete! Now I know what the dentists are up against, no?" ✦ At last they stopped under a tree to consider their dilemma. ✦ Claude sat, chewing a stalk of grass despondently, as his magnificent and self-cleaning inheritance licked its paws. Then Claude suddenly got an idea. ✦ "I know what I'll do," he said. "I'll cook the cat and eat him with a bit of wine sauce! Then I'll set out into the world to find a real fortune!" ✦ And he became quite excited at the prospect of it.

ut the cat, upon hearing these grim remarks, became rather upset, and he immediately began to think of ways to escape his horrible fate—for he knew, as any cat knows, that cats are no more possessed of nine lives than is a clay pitcher.

✦ No sooner had his Master begun to get up than the tomcat leapt in front of him.

✦ "Wait a moment, my friend," he said. "You don't want to eat me! Look, I am nothing but skin and bones! Honest! Besides, how could you kill me after all I did for your papa? It's perfectly obvious that I'm more valuable alive than dead. And just to prove my point, I'll make you a proposal. If in one year's time you are not living in a castle and married to a princess, then you can eat me. Fair enough, *n'est-ce pas*?"

✦ But Claude wasn't convinced.

✦ "I tell you what," the cat continued, "if I fail, I'll even eat my hat! And then you can still eat me!"

✦ Now, of course the cat had no hat, but the Master immediately promised to buy him one, along with a satchel and a pair of boots, and the bargain was struck.

nd thus, properly outfitted, the clever pussycat—now taking the name Puss in Boots—began his plan. ⚜ Now the first thing he did was to get his paws on some nice, green lettuce. He then proceeded to a rabbit's warren in the woods, put the open sack of lettuce on the ground next to himself and pretended to be dead. And sure enough, a stupid young rabbit fell for his trick.

⚜ "Hello there!" said the rabbit upon seeing Puss in Boots. "It, uh, looks like that there kitty is dead. I guess I'll just help myself to some of that there lettuce he's got in his bag. Uhhh,yup!" ⚜ The rabbit then reached in to grab the lettuce, and Puss in Boots quickly closed up the sack and caught him inside.

He then ran to the king's palace and, pretending that his Master was someone of great importance, he presented his catch to the king himself. ⚜ "A gift to His Royal Highness from...from...er... uh... from the Marquis of Carabas!" ⚜ Of course he made the name up on the spot, but the king was so charmed at receiving the gift that he didn't seem to notice. ⚜ "The Marquis of Carabas, you say?" said the king. "Hmm...I've never heard of the good fellow, but please do thank him for me. You see, I do love rabbit very much. In fact, I love rabbit almost as much as I love partridge." ⚜ Well, this last remark gave the cat another idea

and in no time he was practicing his old tricks on a couple of dimwitted partridges in a wheat field:*"Alouette, gentille alouette, alouette, je te plumerai!"* ⚜ And with that they stepped into the bag and were immediately captured and transported to the king's palace.

ow this ruse went on for several months, and as time passed, the gifts became more and more extravagant. ⚜ Finally, as good luck would have it, Puss in Boots learned that the king planned to take his lovely daughter, the princess, for an excursion along the river bank. ⚜ This was precisely what Puss in Boots had been hoping, and he immediately went to his Master with the next phase of his plan. ⚜ "All right. This thing is in the bag, no? You're practically a millionaire already. All you have to do is go swimming in the river at noon tomorrow. Leave the rest to me!" ⚜ And so the lad, who always took a bath once a year whether he needed it or not, complied.

As he was bathing, sure enough, around noontime, the king's carriage drove past. And just as it did, Puss in Boots leapt out of the bushes. ✦ "Help! Help!!" he shouted. "The Marquis of Carabas is drowning! Help!!" ✦ Now the king immediately recognized Puss in Boots and he ordered that the carriage be stopped.

✦ While the king's lackeys were pulling the confused Claude out of the water, Puss in Boots yelled out again: "Stop thief! Stop!"

✦ He then explained to the king that robbers had just then stolen the Marquis' clothes! At once the king commanded the keepers of his wardrobe to go and select the finest suit of clothes he had and give it to the beleaguered Marquis.

hey then brought the Marquis into the carriage, where he was introduced to the king's lovely daughter, who immediately took a liking to him, although he was too shy to speak with her. ⚜ Puss in Boots, seeing that his plan was working, doffed his cap, bid them all *adieu*, and went on ahead. ⚜ A little ways on he came to a field of mowers. ⚜ "Pssst! *Hallo!*" he said to get their attention. "Listen, gentlemen. Tell me the truth. You hate this job, no?" ⚜ "*Oui!*" they responded. ⚜ "And the wages you are paid are too low, no?" he continued. ⚜ "*Oui!!*" they said again. ⚜ "Well," continued Puss in Boots, "I'll make you a deal. If you say that this field belongs to the wonderful Marquis of Carabas when somebody asks you, I'll see to it that the Marquis of Carabas himself gets you a job in his castle at three times what you are making here! *D'accord?*" ⚜ "*Oui, oui...! D'accord, d'accord!!*" said the mowers. ⚜ And the deal was struck.

nd so when the carriage pulled up to the field of mowers, sure enough the curious king stuck his head out. ✦ "Can you tell me to whom this field belongs?" he asked. ✦ "To the wonderful Marquis of Carabas!" they shouted. "It belongs to the wonderful, to the magnificent Marquis of Carabas!" ✦ "My, my," said the king to the young Marquis, "you have certainly inherited a very fine estate. And such a reputation! Even your hired hands speak of you with great admiration." ✦ The Marquis was at that moment staring at his shoes. "Er, uh, I have?" he answered. ✦ "Why, yes. And

I should think you'd be very happy owning such fine property," the king continued. "Very happy indeed!" ✦ "Uh, *oui*, but of course," said the Marquis. And he scratched his head, wondering why his father had never told him of it.

*P*uss in Boots continued running on ahead until he came to a magnificent castle. He knew that a horrible ogre lived there and he decided to pay a visit and investigate the situation. But the ogre was not a very friendly host. ✦ "Tell me, good sir," said Puss in Boots. "I have heard of an ogre in this area who can transform himself into any creature he wants. Er... you wouldn't happen to know which ogre that might be, would you? He is perhaps a friend of yours, no?" ✦ At this the ogre became very angry. ✦ "What!" he said. "Why, I'm the only ogre anywhere in France who possesses that ability. Friend of mine, indeed! Observe, *Monsieur* silly cat!"

Now the ogre's talents were a bit rusty and it took him a few tries before he accomplished his goal. But in time he had indeed transformed himself into a roaring lion. ⚜ This was a development that Puss in Boots hadn't anticipated. He became so frightened that he immediately sprang out of the nearest open window and onto the tile roof outside: "Sometimes, I hate this job!"

When the ogre finally resumed his former appearance, Puss in Boots returned to him. ❧ "That was, eh, *très* impressive," he said to his protean host. "Of course, I don't suppose you could turn yourself into anything a little, how shall we say, smaller, could you? Like, say... a little tiny mouse, for instance?" ❧ "So you don't suppose I'm able to do it, eh?" bellowed the ogre. "All right, smarty, what do you call this?" ❧ He then snapped his fingers and immediately became a tiny brown mouse.

And Puss in Boots, sensing an opportunity, immediately pounced on the mouse and ate it up. ❧ "Gulp. Definitely needs salt." ❧ As soon as he had digested the ogre, Puss in Boots heard the royal coach approaching the castle and he ran outside to meet it. ❧ "Ahem," he said, sweeping his hat in front of him, "welcome to the castle of the Marquis of Carabas!"

"My goodness," said the king, upon seeing the magnificent castle. "*Zut alors! C'est fantastique!*" You see, he was quite impressed. ⚜ "May I have your permission to enter and admire the interior of your magnificent home as well?" ⚜ "But, of course," replied the discombobulated Marquis, "why not?" ⚜ "I have never seen such an impressive castle!" the king said to the Marquis. "Surely you are too modest in not boasting of it! I have never met anyone as modest as you!! You have more to boast of than anyone and yet you act as though you were hardly aware of it. Such tremendous modesty is a rare thing, nowadays!

And in France!! *Impossible*!!!"
⚜ But the modest Marquis only stuck his finger in his ear.

*O*nce inside the king was more impressed than ever and he secretly hoped to bring some of this splendor to his lovely daughter. ✦ "It would seem a terrible shame you have not a wife with whom to share such a home," he said to the Marquis.

"Would it not?" ✦ Puss in Boots had been waiting a long time to hear these words and he watched the Marquis' lips for a response. ✦ But the Marquis was at that moment focused largely on a plaster cherub above his head. ✦ "Uh, I guess so," he replied. ✦ "You guess so?" said the king, puzzled. ✦ At this Puss in Boots gave his Master a subtle and well-placed pinch, by way of encouragement. ✦ "*Waaaaaaaa...* I mean, *oui!* It would seem a shame, wouldn't it? Terrible not to have a wife, absolutely dreadful! Couldn't be worse! Really it couldn't!" ✦ That was all the king needed to hear.

The Marquis and the king's lovely daughter were married within the week! ⚜ Of course, Puss in Boots stayed on in an advisory capacity, and the three of them lived there quite happily for many, many years. ⚜ And if you will believe the little man who is the current caretaker of the ancient castle, it has remained miraculously free of mice and ogres until this very day.